Trapped in Battle Royale
Book Four

THE SQUAD OF LUCKY LANDING

AN UNOFFICIAL FORTNITE NOVEL

Devin Hunter

Sky Pony Press
New York

Sky Pony Press books may be purchased in bulk at special discounts for sales promotion, corporate gifts, fund-raising, or educational purposes. Special editions can also be created to specifications. For details, contact the Special Sales Department, Sky Pony Press, 307 West 36th Street, 11th Floor, New York, NY 10018 or info@skyhorsepublishing.com.

Sky Pony® is a registered trademark of Skyhorse Publishing, Inc.®, a Delaware corporation.

Visit our website at www.skyponypress.com.

10 9 8 7 6 5 4 3 2 1

Library of Congress Cataloging-in-Publication Data is available on file.

Cover art by Amanda Brack
Series design by Brian Peterson

Paperback ISBN: 978-1-5107-4346-5
E-book ISBN: 978-1-5107-4347-2

Printed in Canada

CHAPTER 1

Grey and his squad had made it to the top fifteen in this battle, but the safe zone was growing small as they fortified their position just outside Lucky Landing. They had beaten other squads to the center of the circle, thanks to their landing choice at Fatal Fields. "How's everybody on mats?"

"Still max wood," Kiri said.

"I'm low," Finn admitted. It hadn't been a week since Grey's best friend in real life, Finn, arrived in this hacked virtual reality version of Fortnite Battle Royale. While it was good to have Finn's skills, Grey felt even more responsibility to get them back to the real world.

"Take some of mine," Kiri said as she pulled

materials out of her inventory for Finn to pick up. "No time to farm."

"Nope," Hazel said as she peered through a slat in one of their wooden walls. There was a point when Grey never thought he could work with the mean, trolling Hazel, but so far she had been a big help to the squad. "Four coming from the north."

"Three from the west, too," Grey said as he watched the other side. "This will be tricky."

The games had been changing over the past several days. Grey had a feeling it was due to how close the end of the season was. They only had about twenty days left, and everyone still in contention for the top five spots was playing more cautiously.

Previously, the battles would only last long enough for the storm to shrink three or four times. Now they went on until the safe zone was barely a speck the map. Grey couldn't imagine making it long enough that the storm completely closed in, but he knew that could happen. Finn and Hazel had experienced it when they played in the real world. In that case, whoever died in the storm last was the winner.

The incoming players opened fire on Grey's squad, and Grey replaced the walls as they broke. At least one player had a rocket launcher. Grey had grown to hate those—they destroyed his structures too quickly.

"What's the plan, boss?" Hazel asked.

"Get out." Grey opened a wall on the back side of their tower and jumped out. They were sitting ducks in there, and it didn't look like either team was turning on each other. "Keep an eye out for Tae Min—we are not getting sniped this time."

"At least not until the end," Finn said with a grumble. After some time in the game, Finn had finally learned why everyone was afraid of Tae Min.

Tae Min eliminated Yuri by head shot.

Tae Min eliminated Vlad.

"And there he is," Kiri said. "Too bad we don't know where Yuri and Vlad are."

"They're a duo," Grey said, "so they're not behind us at least."

Grey and his squad ran into Lucky Landing since the safe zone was still well over the southernmost area on the map. They didn't get to come down there often because it was so hard to stay in the safe zone, but Grey had always liked it. Though the game had gone long, the place had been left unlooted because no one came down there.

Even better, a supply drop had fallen right in the courtyard. The supply balloons carrying a box of goods fell later in the game, and they could have fantastic weapons and supplies in them.

"Boxing in," Finn reported as he laid down protective walls.

Kiri did the honors of opening the box, and out popped a glowing orange miracle—a legendary rocket launcher. Now they could be the ones exploding their opponents' structures.

Grey smiled. "Hazel, will you be our explosives expert this game?"

"Yes, please." Hazel grabbed the rocket launcher, and everyone handed over their ammo to her.

And it was just in time, because the enemy squads closed in on them. Grey directed his squad to move into the buildings. If they were going to take rocket-launcher damage, he didn't want to waste their materials building until the opponents ran out of ammo. Their enemies could waste those rockets breaking down Lucky Landing and not Grey's towers.

"Where are we on traps? I have three," Grey said.

"Two here," Finn said. "We building a trap box?"

"Maybe, if they push in." Grey and his squad had climbed to the top level of the building they were in, and he put up walls at lightning speed.

At least one squad had claimed a house across from them, and he'd lost sight of the other one. But he heard walls being broken, so he assumed they were coming in from below. "Finn, block off the stairs. If they come up, use your traps."

"Got it." Finn moved backward to follow Grey's orders.

The squad in the other house opened fire on the tower Grey had built out of the Lucky Landing structure. He could tell they were only testing them, though, because they could have busted down the walls much faster. Maybe they didn't want to waste ammo.

"Hazel, time for rockets. Kiri, pick off whoever you see." Grey had his building blueprints out, and he used the edit tool to open a small window for Hazel to shoot rockets out of. Then he built higher up, trusting Kiri would know to follow him to a better sniper position.

Kiri did. They climbed several ramps higher and from their new perch unloaded fire onto the now-exposed enemy squad.

Hazel knocked down Zach.

Kiri eliminated Ben.

Grey knocked down Tristan.

Grey smiled. They didn't beat Ben and

Tristan's new squad often, but it was always a welcome occurrence when they did. "Keep up the pressure. Hui Yin is still up."

"More rockets on the way," Hazel replied as her rockets continued to soar into what could hardly be called a building anymore.

Hazel eliminated Hui Yin.

With the last enemy squad member eliminated, all the downed players were eliminated as well. Now Grey turned his attention to the squad coming from below. "How you doing down there, Finn?"

"Traps didn't work. They haven't come up the stairs," he replied. "I heard their footsteps, but I can't tell where they went."

"Got it." Grey had a feeling Finn dropped the traps too soon, even though Grey had said to drop them *after* Finn spotted the players on the stairs. You couldn't get away with preemptively dropped traps on top players. They were much smarter than lower-ranked enemies. "My bet is it's Lam's squad then. Probably hiding."

Kiri sighed. "They're such turtles."

They were, but they were also all ranked in the top ten. Lam's squad never prioritized eliminations—they farmed mats and hid out for as long as they could. But that didn't mean they should be counted out. They knew the late game better than anyone, and they had a way of trapping their opponents in builds. Grey had taken to watching Lam sometimes after he was eliminated, and she was a master at making a labyrinth to impede enemies and ultimately destroy them.

It wasn't a flashy play style, but it got the job done.

"We gotta be careful," Grey said as he looked at the map for the next circle. They were just outside of it, and he was certain they would make sure to be there first with only a few people left on the map. "How many rockets do we have left?"

"Five," Hazel said.

"Save them until we find their base." Grey opted to leave their building from his own platforms, assuming Lam's squad might have left their own traps on the way down.

The next safe zone wasn't very far from them and still in Lucky Landing, but as they approached it, Grey saw the fortified building that likely contained Lam's squad. They had built metal walls around one of the southernmost structures, and Grey was nervous to approach. This team was smart and deserving of their top-ten status.

"What should we do?" Finn asked as he built their own protective walls.

No one shot back as he did this. Grey didn't like that. Usually a team would go on the offensive if they already had the high ground and fortifications. Lam's squad wanted you to come to them, which had to mean they had a plan to destroy you.

"Why aren't they shooting?" Hazel asked. "They had to have heard us. They must see us."

"I don't know." Grey looked behind them, worrying that they were so focused on Lam's squad that Tae Min would sneak up on them. "Watch for Tae Min, Kiri. I have a feeling we're surrounded."

"No doubt." Kiri turned away from the big building, her sniper scope out.

"Permission to approach the tower," Finn said. "We're already top ten for the game—I'm good with that."

"You sure? You need the ranks the most," Grey said.

Finn shrugged. "This is getting annoying. Let's get it over with."

Grey was at a loss for how to approach, so he said, "Okay, you go first. Me and Hazel will fake push behind you."

"Going." Finn ran forward, building ramps and walls to protect himself. But no one shot at him.

Just when Grey was beginning to think the place was abandoned, the explosions started. Finn went down immediately as the entire front wall disintegrated under the C4 that Lam's team had put there. If that wasn't smart enough, there was a *second* structure behind that one with windows built into it. Lam's squad opened fire on Grey and Hazel before Hazel could get off one rocket.

Soon, they were eliminated along with Finn.

Kiri followed soon after, taking a head shot from Tae Min as he entered the safe zone. Lam's team reset their trap, and even Tae Min didn't have the patience to wait them out this time. Their squad took the victory, and the member with the highest eliminations would take the top rank for the game.

"They're so annoying," Finn grumbled after Grey's squad was teleported back to the battle warehouse at the end of their day.

"But smart," Grey replied. Maybe it wasn't a style that anyone liked, but Grey had to admit that what Lam's squad was doing worked for them. He needed to find something equally effective for his squad so they could take over the top five.

CHAPTER 2

Grey's squad finished in the top fifteen at least once a day, and that had been enough to boost their ranks closer to the top twenty. But they still needed more. More top-ten finishes. More Victory Royales. As he looked at their ranks while the Admin did her usual speech, he couldn't help worry that there weren't enough games to do it.

Ben and Tristan were still several ranks above him, and Grey glared at their names. He needed to beat them more often if he wanted to take their ranks.

The Admin disappeared before Grey even thought to listen to her. His squad mates gathered around him, probably ready for his usual decision on what they'd be practicing before their mandatory rest time.

"What's the plan?" Finn bounced on his toes, already prepared to play more. He hadn't tired one bit of the game. In fact, he sometimes complained that they only got to play five battles a day. He'd played much more than that in the real world. "Should we find a squad to practice with? Some duos?"

Grey shook his head.

He looked over to where Lam and her squad were. She was much older than Grey, he guessed twenty-five, with shoulder-length black hair. There were only three in Lam's squad, Pilar and Trevor being the others, and they whispered amongst themselves before heading outside. He knew not to ask them for practice. They worked alone. It seemed like a lot of the top teams said that. Yuri and Vlad also rejected practice. It sounded like recently, Zach's squad had also stopped practicing with Hans's squad.

People were moving into end-game phase. No one wanted to share strategies or show off their true skills.

Maybe Grey's squad should consider that as well. "Let's have a . . . meeting."

Finn raised an eyebrow. "A meeting?"

Grey nodded. "In the forest."

Grey began to walk, and they followed him in silence for awhile. It didn't seem like anyone else was among the trees, but he kept an ear out just in case.

Before they stopped, Hazel said, "We're not in trouble, are we? You're not gonna leave us for Lam's squad or something."

Grey whirled around in surprise. "No! Why would you say that?"

Hazel folded her arms. "You always say they're smart . . . and you'd fit in with them with all your tactical skills."

"Well, I've never even talked to them," Grey said. "I wanted to talk about strategy—the top squads are keeping more to themselves as we get closer to the end of the season, and the battles are slowing down. I wanted your opinions, but I didn't want other players overhearing us."

"Oh." Hazel ran a hand through her short green hair. "That's a valid concern. The games are getting weird. More defensive."

"I have a feeling it'll only get worse," Kiri said. "Everyone is more careful—I'm not getting nearly as many snipes once we get past the top thirty."

"People are playing boring." Finn leaned on a tree, looking sullen. "I wish I was here back at the beginning of the season when people were probably trying to get more eliminations."

"Boring is relative," Grey said. "I want you all to have fun, but I want to help us all get home even more. That has always been my goal, with you guys and the guys from our old squad. And to do that, we have to start thinking about the end game and being top ten as many times as possible. We need to consider all the options for winning. I know people look down on Lam's squad for being turtles, but they are top ten and that's where we want to be, right?"

Hazel sighed. "Yeah, it's true. We have to figure out how to beat their crazy tactics at least."

"We also need to find them early to tank their ranks," Kiri said.

"They might be good builders but not great fighters," Finn offered.

"Okay, good, this is what I wanted—let's brainstorm what we can do to pull down the squads that outrank us." Grey took a seat under the nearest tree, and everyone joined him. "I don't care if the tactic is cheap, boring, or whatever. We're getting to the point where we can't have pride in how we win."

"Well, then explosives are the way to go," Finn said. "Those things are so overpowered. Look how Lam popped me with those C4. Rockets and grenades are good, too. We should have a big stock of those for pushing."

"If we can find them," Kiri said. "It's not like we get explosives every game."

"Of course, but we can save them for late game when we do get them," Finn replied. "Getting that rocket launcher really helped us out this game."

"For sure." Grey agreed that explosives were becoming increasingly important, especially in the end game. "So we can all agree that we should build strategies around explosives. We can't assume we're the only ones thinking these will be clutch. We'll need to come up with countermeasures as well. And hopefully some creative ways to use them, like how Lam's squad baited us. It was cheap, but clever, too. We can't complain when it's a fair fight and they outsmart us."

Everyone nodded in agreement.

"Okay, what else?" Grey didn't want to be the

only one coming up with plans—he had learned it was important for his squad to have ideas as well. Sometimes he would freeze up. If other people contributed, they all had a better chance at winning.

"I hate it, but building seems to be more and more clutch," Hazel admitted. "Not just the fast building, but all that *editing*. Like how they had windows on their walls and were ready to shoot."

Grey nodded. "Or players cut their stairs in half, or make a small hole in the floor and drop a trap. There's a lot we could figure out there."

"I don't know how people think of that in the moment," Kiri said as she stretched out in the grass under the trees. "Watching others do it is one thing, but I blank and start shooting in hopes of getting someone down."

Finn nodded. "High-pressure situations can be hard to build in."

"There should be a way to practice that, though," Grey said. "Maybe if we put pressure on each other and try new things to get out of it. Non-shooting things."

"Can't hurt, but do you really think we can make top five? It seems like a long shot at this point." Hazel wore a concerned expression on her face. While she still wasn't the nicest person on the planet, Grey appreciated that she was upfront and not afraid to bring up issues. In a lot of ways, it actually helped them get better.

"It's not," Grey said, though a little voice inside whispered that Hazel had a point. "We just have to keep ranking higher, and we can do that. It might not be flashy, but I know we can if we work hard and target the players above us in rank. We have to come up with ways to stop them from succeeding."

Hazel gave a smile that Grey knew as her "troll grin." "Sabotage, eh?"

The word made Grey feel gross inside. "Not necessarily . . . More like coming up with strategies that directly ruin theirs. We can't play their games—we need them to play ours."

Hazel frowned. "You're no fun."

"I want to get home and get you guys there, too, but it's gotta be fair. We fight in the battles, not outside." Grey shrugged. "Sorry if it's not fun. Blame whoever trapped us here, not me."

"This isn't a trap," Finn said. "It's heaven."

"Maybe it would be if we could go back and forth," Hazel said.

Grey decided to overlook Finn's comment.

His best friend would realize he wanted to go home at some point, and Grey would make sure he had the ranking to do it. "Let's try practicing under pressure. Figuring out how to react fast never hurts."

"I'm down," Kiri said as she stood up. "To the practice area!"

They all headed in that direction, and Grey tried to think of ways he could test his squad mates. He'd need every ounce of creativity he had left to help them rank up before the end of the season.

CHAPTER 3

Every new day of battling brought Grey more and more stress. It was one more day he had to do well. One less day he had to improve. As they gathered in the battle warehouse to start the day, Grey told himself they'd had a good practice last night. It was all he could do before the Admin arrived and they were teleported to the line that placed them in their rank.

"Welcome to Day Forty of Battles!" the Admin said with her usual cheer. "I am excited to announce that there will be another patch in the coming days!"

"Already?" someone near him whispered. "But we just had one . . ."

"Unlike previous patches, this one holds a

special event that will happen at an undisclosed time after the patch," the Admin continued. "The rocket previously placed in the mountain base will be launched, and it will take place during one of your coming battles. Once that rocket launches, several changes will take place leading up to the next season.

"While I will not disclose those changes, I will detail the alterations that are effective immediately after the patch. Shotguns will receive a twenty percent decrease in their damage and accuracy. There will also be a delay in shooting added when a player switches between two shotguns in their inventory—"

"What?" Jamar yelled from the line. "That's crap! You're basically making the double pump useless!"

"It was too overpowered anyway," Hans called from his own spot in the line.

"You may discuss the patch changes in your free time," the Admin said. "Please, no further interruptions. I have a lot of information to divulge."

The Admin wasn't kidding. She went over every detail of the upcoming patch, and it was much longer than the last patch Grey experienced.

And it seemed a lot worse. Shotguns took a big hit, but for some reason they were introducing another SMG-category weapon that could carry more ammo in a round before having to reload. They were also introducing a dual pistol that sounded interesting.

Rocket launchers took a hit—having their ammo maxed out at twelve shots that you could carry total. While Grey knew having a huge stack of rockets was overpowered, this was still disappointing. That weapon had made games for them, and now they would have to be much more careful with how they used their ammo.

Traps also took a damage reduction, making it so they wouldn't instantly down a player if they got hit with one. By the time the Admin got through all the tweaks and changes, Grey's head was spinning with the new information. He tried to put it all together in his head, but it was too much. The Admin needed to give them a reference guide to look at after all that.

"This will be the last and biggest patch before the new season," the Admin said. "For those who stay, prepare yourselves for more exciting changes. Good luck in today's battles!"

The Admin vanished, and people barely had

time to talk before the first battle began. But they still tried, most of them in a frenzy over all the changes.

Grey's vision went black, and the next thing he knew he was on the Battle Bus flying over the island that held his fate. He checked the map, finding the bus was flying north over the eastern side of the island.

"All those changes are gonna be crazy!" Finn said. "They're gonna launch the rocket? I wonder what it'll do!"

"Maybe it'll make another crater like Dusty Divot," Hazel offered. "I still miss the old Dusty Depot sometimes."

"Me too," Finn said. "But it would be cool to have new locations on the map! Some places are basically useless and no one ever goes there."

"So true," Hazel said. "Like Moisty Mire."

"Or Haunted Hills," Finn replied.

Grey and Kiri had nothing to say since they had only played the game as long as they'd been stuck in it. Grey knew nothing of past seasons or big changes to the map. And he didn't want to find out, either. Because finding out what the next patches held would mean he'd be stuck there a whole extra season.

"Let's try Shifty Shafts," Grey said. "It's good for loot and close to Tilted Towers. Maybe some top teams will be there to farm up and we can take them out early."

"I'm game," Finn said.

"If it looks too hot," Grey said as he jumped from the bus, "go to Greasy Grove instead."

Most of the players jumped from the Battle Bus early, and Grey watched as a heavy portion glided their way to Tilted Towers and the surrounding areas. Grey was still afraid to land in Tilted Towers because of the high risk. Either players survived by eliminating everyone else or they died early. While it looked like a fun place to play, he couldn't risk low-ranked games at this point.

There was at least one other squad landing in Shifty Shafts, but Grey held his ground because he thought they could win. If it had been more, it could have been too dangerous. "Grab weapons first. Call if you need backup."

Grey landed on top of a ragged house and broke the roof to get inside. Someone was right behind him, so instead of going for the chest, he grabbed the basic shotgun that was lying on the ground with ammo. He turned and shot. He hit the player and downed her before running for the chest.

You knocked down Mayumi.

"It's Hans's squad!" Grey called out. "Be careful!" Shotguns were slow enough to reload as it was—he needed whatever weapon was in that chest if more enemies were coming to revive their squad mate.

Footsteps sounded somewhere in the house, indicating that someone was definitely on their way to attempt to save Mayumi. Grey had noted that she'd crawled behind some boxes in attempts to hide. He opened the chest as he said, "I might need backup."

"On my way," Finn said.

Grey picked up the green AR and the small shield potions that came out of the chest. There was also clinger grenades. He'd save those for later if he could.

You eliminated Mayumi.

Not wanting to take chances, he decided it was better to make sure Mayumi ranked low than to save the ammo for whoever was about to attack. He had just enough, and Finn was on his way from the abandoned mine section of the area. Someone was breaking down the floor from

below, and Grey hurriedly gathered what material he could from the debris lying around the
attic. He had just enough wood for two walls,
but it was better than nothing.

"Two on me!" Finn said as shots sounded outside. "Sorry, Grey. Now I need backup."

"Almost there," Hazel said.

"I'll handle it," Grey replied as he chugged
two of his small shields. He was tempted to use
his clingers, but he went back to his shotgun in
hopes to get a good initial shot. Chances were,
the player didn't have a full shield or any at all. A
head shot would go a long way.

The floor broke, and the enemy emerged
blasting an SMG. Grey took two hits before he
threw up a wall for protection. The wall melted
under the constant pressure of the SMG. Grey
had to throw up a second with the remainder of
his materials.

Forget saving them. Grey switched back to his
clinger grenades. He couldn't get eliminated this
early. Once his wall went down, Grey threw a
grenade, and it stuck to the player wearing the
pink bearskin. He could sense their panic, and
he was sure the player didn't have a shield at all.
The pink bear ran toward him, knowing that the

grenade would damage the thrower if they were close enough.

Grey ran for the opening in the attic and jumped out of the house. The clinger exploded, and with it came the notification: *You knocked down Rafael.*

"You got the others?" Grey asked as he ran toward his squad mates' icons on the minimap. They were on the dirt road between the house and the mine, fighting around a makeshift structure. It wasn't very tall, since no one had had time to farm materials, but it was enough to offer protection for both teams.

Hazel had taken some damage, and Kiri had taken too much for this early on. They needed to get the rest of Hans's squad down before it was too late. Grey added his AR shots from the side, knowing that if they could get the remaining two down then Rafael would be eliminated as well.

Grey got some damage down on the player wearing the T-Rex skin, but they turned on him immediately. He had to duck behind the house, only at half health now. He chugged his remaining shields and tried to get in more shots.

"I'm almost out of ammo," Finn warned.

"Me too," Hazel said.

"I *am* out," Kiri replied. She had already backed away from the fight and had moved into the mines in search of more loot. "But T-Rex is one hit, I swear."

"Okay, I'm using my clingers," Grey announced.

Grey chucked his remaining two clinger grenades at the enemies, knowing they wouldn't hurt his squad mates though they would hurt Grey. A weird quirk of the game. One stuck to the T-Rex, and the other stuck to the build.

You have knocked down Farrah.

You have knocked down Hans.

With the whole squad knocked down, the next notifications read that all those people had been eliminated by Grey. Maybe he'd used the explosives too early, but he had four eliminations to his name and a high-ranked squad eliminated on top of it.

"Ouch, they're ranked in the eighties," Finn said. "That'll hurt their standing."

"We gotta keep doing that," Grey said. "Farm it up."

Grey broke down everything he could for materials, and they looted the rest of Shifty

Shafts. It was a decent haul of weapons and other items, but he still didn't feel like it would be enough if they met a good squad.

The first circle was pushing them toward Tilted Towers, but Grey was afraid to go there. Whoever had survived the initial chaos had to be geared up like crazy. But at the same time, whoever survived was probably a top team.

And they needed those top teams to take early losses.

Grey took a deep breath. "Okay, guys, we're going to Tilted. Keep your eyes out."

"A-Are you sure?" Kiri sounded as nervous as Grey felt.

"Either we start taking out high rankers early or we may as well be done," Grey replied.

"Yeah! Let's do this!" Finn was already rushing for Tilted Towers. It was his favorite spot, and he constantly begged Grey to go there. "No risk, no reward!"

"Up the mountain," Grey replied. If they were going into such a dangerous area, they at least needed to take the high ground. The mountain between Shifty Shafts and Tilted Towers would put them above the city. That way, they could get a good look down into the towers and streets to see what they might be dealing with.

As they climbed the steep mountain, breaking down trees for materials as they went, the sounds of battle grew louder. Grey peeked over the top of the mountain, and below he saw a mess of fighting. Winding builds, loot scattering from those eliminated, and still there were at least two squads battling.

A couple weeks ago, this scenario would have frozen Grey in place. While he was still nervous, he told himself they had the advantage. They were going in fresh. They could take the enemy by surprise.

"Here we go!" Grey began to lay down floors from the mountain into the middle of Tilted Towers. He told himself he could win this fight, and he almost believed it.

CHAPTER 4

As Grey and his squad pressed in on the other enemy groups, he tried to assess who was weakest. He wanted to take them out first and then focus on the others. Chances were, Grey's squad had far more materials to build with than these two squads—Grey had the advantage.

The enemies fought around the big gray tower some called "Castle Tower." Grey expected the squads to run inside for cover even though he didn't want that to happen. Those towers were narrow with lots of stairs, and getting stuck in close quarters seemed to be the easiest way to be eliminated in Tilted Towers.

"Dudes on the left are low," Finn announced.

Grey trusted it. Even if Grey couldn't tell which players were low on health, Finn had a knack for keeping track of who got hit. "Let's push them then."

Continuing to build over to the tower, Grey made sure to connect their build to the surrounding structures so that the other squads wouldn't knock them down. Hazel kept up pressure, as did Finn, while Kiri watched their back for any other enemies.

Finn knocked down Ben.

"Yes!" Grey said with excitement. It *was* another high-ranking team here, and if Grey's squad could get them down early, that would benefit his rank. "Throw all the pressure down— I'll handle the defense."

"Aye, aye, captain!" Kiri said as she used her hunting rifle to take aim at the remaining players in Zach's squad.

Kiri knocked down Hui Yin.

Lam knocked down Tristan.

"Crap, it's Lam's squad, too!" Hazel said as the other enemy pressed in to clean up the eliminations on Zach's squad.

Grey was honestly surprised to see them, since they usually hid out until late game. He didn't think Lam would land in Tilted Towers. Maybe she hadn't—maybe they'd dropped in after farming like Grey had. "Watch out for them. They probably have the mats to fight."

"Bet they came in from the north, based on their build," Finn said.

"Boxing in." Grey built brick walls around them. He needed a moment to consider how to face them because there were still fifty players left in this battle. He wanted a higher rank than that. "Anyone got traps?"

"I grabbed two. Here." Hazel dropped the traps.

Grey picked them up. "Thanks. We're gonna pretend to run, okay? Then trap the way down. They don't have explosives—they'd have used them by now on this giant build."

"Got it," Finn said. "I have a bouncer if we get into a sticky spot."

"Great. Let's move." Grey descended into the castle tower below them. He wasn't sure if Lam's squad would follow, but he was prepared for them. Only the sound of his own squad's footsteps sounded for a few seconds, but then he heard the pounding of more players. So Lam's squad would pursue them.

"Staircase," Grey said.

"That's suicide!" Kiri replied.

"I have a plan, I swear." Grey hadn't had the opportunity to use this particular trick before, but he had thought about it. As his squad crowded into the cramped staircase, Grey put a wall behind them, and then he placed a trap on the ceiling. "Keep going down."

As Grey placed more walls to block off the stairs, the footsteps grew louder above them. He was sure Lam's squad would see the wall and trap.

And that was the point.

"Put your bounce pad under the staircase," Grey instructed to Finn. "They'll probably destroy that trap and the stairs, thinking there could be more traps. Then I'll drop my other one above them."

"I'll die laughing if this works." Finn placed his bouncer down just as the sound of weapons shooting filled the space. Grey couldn't see where they were shooting, but he heard the first trap break. He pulled out the second trap and hoped for the best.

The staircase above the bounce pad began to shake and crumble as it took damage, and Grey's heart raced as he worked to find the right angle to lay down the trap. "Open fire when they drop, for good measure."

His squad mates aimed their weapons. The staircase broke, and down came Lam's squad onto the bounce pad. Grey frantically threw the trap as his squad let shots fly. The trap set, and out came the spikes. Combined with the damage from his team's barrage, Lam's squad didn't have a chance. They were all downed and then eliminated immediately after.

Finn's laugh filled the coms. "I can't believe that worked!"

"Lam underestimated you after that last battle," Hazel said. "Don't expect it to work again."

"I won't." Grey and his squad mates went through the loot. Lam's squad had a lot of mats, enough to fill Grey to full in each category and leave some for everyone else, too. "That's three top-twenty squads out early. Let's make the most of this."

"Heck yeah!" Finn's avatar danced their victory, the music sounding throughout the building.

"No dancing!" Grey said. "What have I told you about dancing before a win?"

Finn stopped. "That it'll put a target on our—"

A loud sniper shot echoed through Tilted Towers, and the shot flew through the window and hit Finn for almost all his shield and health.

Grey reflexively used walls to protect them, but he almost wanted to leave Finn to his fate. He dropped his med kit for Finn. "See? No dancing!"

Several more shots flew at them while Finn healed up, but Grey blocked them with walls. He even added a ramp so the person would have to get through two things before hitting anyone.

"It's probably Tae Min," Kiri said. "We'll never make top ten with him on our tails."

Given the pinpoint accuracy and the fact that the player didn't seem to have backup, Grey assumed Kiri had guessed right. "We'll have to outrun him. Maybe he'll find someone else to bother."

"How do we outrun Tae Min?" Hazel asked. "We don't have a launchpad or bouncers. And he's probably running right for us."

"Then we better move." Grey ran not for the stairs, but for a window on the opposite side of the building from where the shooting had originated. He jumped out and took to the ground.

"Don't rely on me for shield walls here. If you see him, protect yourself."

His squad's avatars all pulled out their blueprints, meaning they were in build mode and ready. The next storm circle would push them more towards the east and Loot Lake. They were about to get pinched between a bunch of squads and Tae Min.

He was pretty sure having Tae Min at their backs was worse.

"We need to get other people between us and Tae Min," Grey said. "Otherwise this is over."

"Or we could just eliminate him," Finn said.

Kiri scoffed. "Have you gone crazy? Has he not eliminated you enough yet?"

"Everyone *always* runs from him!" Finn snapped back. "We're a squad of *four people* running away from one guy. That's what's crazy."

"The kid is right," Hazel said. "But he just doesn't realize squads run because Tae Min is that good."

Both of them had a point, though Grey wasn't sure now was the right time to test it. "The problem is he's hard to spot and good at keeping cover until he finds the right opening. But look, Finn, if you spot him . . . we can try to put pressure on him and see where it goes."

"Deal," Finn said.

"He has the blond-dude default skin this round," Kiri said. "Saw it through my scope."

"We'd only be throwing away our ranking . . ." Hazel grumbled.

"We got three top teams down!" Finn replied. "We've got to be more confident."

Grey's squad moved to the other side of the lake without much incident. As the storm closed in again, more people were eliminated as they tried to get into the safe zone. Grey's squad picked off a few enemies that came in from the storm, but it was no one particularly threatening. They would have to look out for Vlad and Yuri, though, since Grey hadn't seen them on the list of eliminations yet. Hazel's old squad was also still in the game, as well as Lorenzo's.

It felt easy with some of their toughest competition gone, but Grey didn't want to get complacent. The circle was closing in on the open areas between Loot Lake and Dusty Divot. Grey set his sights on the mountain. "We're getting that high ground first, and we're keeping it for as long as it stays in the circle."

"Sounds like a good plan," Kiri said.

"Kiri, you build up," Grey directed so he could save his own materials.

They followed Kiri up the mountain as she built ramps. Grey scanned the area, hoping no one else had staked out the place yet. He couldn't see anyone there, and there weren't any builds nearby, but they had no view of the opposite side of the mountain yet. Most players would pick the high ground in a fight, so Grey pulled out an SMG and prepared to see others who might challenge them for the top.

Just as they reached the flat peak, the blond default avatar appeared from the opposite side of the mountain.

"Tae Min!" Finn yelled as he opened fire with a shotgun.

Grey used his SMG, and this time it was Tae Min throwing walls to defend himself. "Kiri, build up! I'm not dropping pressure."

"Okay!" Kiri built walls and ramps to protect from Tae Min's return fire.

Once Grey had to reload the SMG, he switched to his AR to keep breaking Tae Min's walls. Hazel had joined in the fire, and all Tae Min could do was try to protect himself. He'd taken at least a few hits from Finn's fast reaction.

Grey wished he still had those clinger grenades—it would be over now if he'd saved those.

Tae Min seemed to have endless materials, and it began to feel like Grey was wasting ammo. He needed to do something. Even if it felt crazy.

"He'll try to heal if we let up," Grey said. "Cover me."

Grey switched to building and added a few more ramps so he could get above the box Tae Min had made for himself. He shot the top off it, and Tae Min replaced it and the wall Grey's teammates shot at.

Growing frustrated, Grey felt like the answer to this situation was right in front of him and he couldn't quite grasp it. Tae Min didn't usually box in for so long—he would find a way to retreat and attack from a different way. Grey began to wonder if this was some kind of test. If it was, Grey was failing.

"How does he replace walls so fast?" Kiri yelled. "Does he have infinite mats?"

That's it. Grey realized what he had to do, and he'd have to do it fast. He shot at the top of Tae Min's box, but instead of breaking it entirely, he waited for the other side to go down. Grey shot the top down at the same time and quickly switched to building himself. He placed a brick wall down before Tae Min could place his own.

Then Grey edited it open and shot down at Tae Min with his SMG.

Grey eliminated Tae Min.

"Yes! We got him!" Finn cheered and hollered over the comms. "See? I told you!"

"You did . . ." Grey was happy to have Tae Min out of the way, but he had a weird feeling that Tae Min let them have that elimination. It didn't seem like Tae Min was doing his best.

The rest of the game went smoothly, and they earned a Victory Royale. Grey was glad to have it, especially when his competition had been eliminated early on. Now they just needed about twenty more games like that and they'd make it to the top five.

CHAPTER 5

Grey had a feeling that after Ben and Tristan got a low rank, they would go to their favorite spot the next game: Fatal Fields. He was right, and his squad was able to take out Ben and Tristan's squad early like the game before. Grey had a hunch they'd go somewhere quiet the next game to farm up, and so he tried for Lucky Landing. They weren't there, but their two squads collided just outside of Moisty Mire.

Grey's won again, having gotten better loot at Lucky Landing.

"What is your deal, man?" Tristan yelled after the third game of the day. He stomped over to Grey, clearly on tilt after several bad finishes in a row. "You're hunting us down now? That's your new plan?"

Grey shrugged. Tristan had no right to be mad about that. When he and Ben left Grey and Kiri, they didn't tell them just to hurt Grey and Kiri's ranking. "Tanking ranks—I learned from the best."

Tristan's face went bright red with anger. "Why can't you pay your dues like a good little noob?"

"Excuse me?" Hazel jumped in, her hands on her hips. "This has nothing to do with paying your dues—it's about skill. You veterans are so entitled!"

"We're entitled?" Tristan said. "You're selfish!"

Ben stomped between the two of them, looking more sad than angry. "Guys, stop! C'mon, Tris, we don't have a right to be mad at them for targeting us. We would do the same thing."

"We *will* do the same thing," Tristan said as he glared at Grey. "You won't get lucky every game."

"Who says it's luck?" Finn chimed in.

Zach, Ben and Tristan's new squad leader, decided to join the conversation. "Save the fire for the battles, okay? No reason to show Grey how tilted he's got you."

Tristan deflated at this. "Sorry, Zach."

"Better not happen again." Zach gave Tristan a disappointed look, and Grey wondered if Zach was already considering removing Ben and Tristan based on a few bad games. Their ranking had dropped below the top ten now. If Grey kept finding them early, he could tank them even further.

A part of him felt guilty for having to hurt Ben's and Tristan's chances of going home, but it was their choice to be his opposition instead of staying on his team.

And Grey knew he could beat them now.

He even believed he could beat everyone with a bit more practice.

Eliminating Tae Min earlier had given him a new sense of confidence, and he'd learned another important skill on the way. Replacing that wall and editing it had changed the way Grey saw building. If he owned a wall or ramp, it meant he was in control of it. He could manipulate it, and thus he could manipulate his opponent, too. New strategies opened up in his mind, and he already felt like he was playing at a higher level than he had the day before.

"Great job so far today, guys," Grey said as

Zach's squad backed off and headed for the practice area.

"We doing more drills?" Finn asked.

Grey shook his head. "I need a mental break. You guys can do what you want."

"Go recharge, mate," Kiri said. "I want a rest, too. Playing like that is exhausting."

"I miss naps," Hazel said. "I'll be in my bed wishing I could sleep."

"Have fun with that," Finn replied. "I'm still gonna practice. See you all in an hour."

"Yup." Grey waved to everyone as he headed off to the forest by the cabins. It had become his favorite place to go when he needed some space from the game. His squad had figured out that sometimes a mental break was more important than practice, and they always took at least one hour to rest during battle time.

Grey walked to the very edge of the forest where there was a barrier that stopped him from going any further. He sat under a tree and closed his eyes, trying to separate his mind from all the strategies it wanted to concoct.

Think of home. It had been almost six weeks since he got trapped in this game, and it felt like his memories were already growing hazy. He could remember his mom's face, but it didn't seem as clear. He knew what his house looked like, but he was beginning to forget what it felt like to live there. These thoughts always made him homesick, but he didn't let it get to him like before.

He used it to fuel his determination to win.

Grey heard footsteps coming toward him, and he opened his eyes to see who it was. He'd assumed it would be a squad mate, so when he spotted Tae Min, he was surprised.

Though Grey wouldn't say he and Tae Min were friends, he was aware that Tae Min didn't talk to hardly anyone. Grey didn't know why Tae Min talked to him, but he always learned something from Tae Min when he did. And he was grateful for that.

Grey summoned his courage to say something first, "You gave us that elimination, didn't you?"

Tae Min sat next to Grey, looking forward at the dense trees. "What makes you say that?"

"You could have built out of that . . ." Grey said. "I don't know, it felt like you were waiting for me to figure out what to do."

A wisp of a smile appeared on Tae Min's face. "Why would I do that?"

Grey shrugged. He wasn't sure if he was right about Tae Min or if he had read the whole situation wrong. It seemed like Tae Min didn't want to tell him the truth, either. Grey didn't know what else to say, so they sat there in silence.

"You are getting better at reading people," Tae Min said after a few moments.

"I had to learn the hard way." Grey's insides twisted as he thought of Ben and Tristan, even his current squad mates. He'd had to figure out how they all worked in order to help them improve . . . and knowing how they worked also meant he could make them stumble as well.

"The hard way is the only way." Tae Min leaned back on his hands and sighed. "You were right, by the way. I wanted to see if you would realize you could replace my wall. You passed the test, though it took you a little too long."

"Test?" Grey gulped. "I didn't realize I was being graded."

"Why would I do that?" Tae Min said again, this time with a bigger smile.

Grey was still afraid to answer that question, though he wanted to say Tae Min was training him to win. Grey couldn't deny it felt like Tae Min wanted to help him get home, but it was too big a thing to say out loud. So Grey asked a question in return. "Is anyone else being tested like me?"

Tae Min let out a small laugh. "I think you know the answer to that question just like you know the answer to the other one. Trust your instincts."

"And then?" Grey asked.

Tae Min stood up. He still hadn't looked directly at Grey. "And then we'll see."

Grey watched Tae Min walk away. Everyone had said that Tae Min picked someone to carry to victory, but if Grey had been chosen, it sure didn't feel like "being carried." He'd been working his butt off trying to get better. Tae Min had given him some advice, sure, but it had always been up to Grey to use it the right way.

Though he didn't think Tae Min was advising anyone else, Grey felt like that was because the other people Tae Min might help were already with Grey. And Grey had been teaching Kiri, Ben, Tristan, Hazel, and Finn with the advice Tae Min had given him.

It was the most efficient for Tae Min to talk to Grey, who would then do the work of training.

Grey shook his head. "So he's testing me, and I'm testing all the other ones for him."

There was a time when Grey would have done anything to be chosen as the one Tae Min carried to victory, but he now saw it wasn't like that at all. Tae Min didn't carry people—he taught people in a way that no one understood. He had given Grey confidence. He'd helped him improve his natural abilities. He'd taught him how to deal with people in the game.

Grey felt a lot of pressure to measure up to whatever Tae Min saw in him, but even if Grey ultimately didn't meet Tae Min's expectations, he still felt like he had a good chance to make it home.

After the last few games, Grey knew his squad could compete with the top players, and he was coming for those ranks.

With or without Tae Min's help.

CHAPTER 6

Over the next two days, Grey's squad won themselves four Victory Royales. As Grey thought about all the practice he'd done with the other top contenders, he realized he knew how to counter their styles. The victories had pushed them up into the top fifteen, and it felt good to finally see some progress. Especially since the new patch would be dropping tomorrow, and that could cause their ranking to take a hit until they adjusted to all the changes.

The only players Grey struggled against were the ones he didn't know as well. Like Lam's squad, whom they were currently fighting for the top spot in their last battle of the day.

Every time Grey figured out one of Lam's

strategies, she would use another he wasn't prepared for. Sometimes Grey's squad got lucky and beat them anyway, but it often went the other way as well.

The circle was smaller than Grey had ever survived to see, and Lam's squad had the high ground in the massive tower they'd built. Grey didn't want to push them, since last time they tried that, Lam used a bounce pad to propel Grey and Finn into the storm. They took so much damage from the storm, they had no hope of survival. Lam's squad easily finished off Kiri and Hazel after that.

"Let's bring it down," Grey finally said. That was his instinct, and as Tae Min said, it had paid off to listen to his gut. "You still got that C4, Hazel?"

"Eight whole charges," she replied.

That was more than enough to bring down the tower. "Glad we saved that."

Hazel placed the C4 on the weakest parts of the tower, and Grey and Finn built ramps down to avoid the fire. Some shots were fired from above, but nothing hit them since they stayed almost directly below Lam's squad. Grey had found it was hard for the high-ground players to hit him if he stuck right below their position.

As Hazel detonated the C4, Grey watched the tower break apart wall by wall. He held his weapon up, expecting Lam's squad to survive. Sure enough, he saw them fly from the top of the structure. They had used a launchpad.

"Shoot them down!" Grey yelled.

He aimed at the enemies, but it was like shooting ants, they were so far away. Grey didn't hit a single shot, but it looked like his squad mates had. A player fell from the sky when Kiri knocked them down, and when they hit the ground, the notification read: *Kiri eliminated Trevor with a great fall.*

"Two more! We got this!" Finn said as he aimed for Lam and her other squad member, Pilar. "The knight skin is one hit from down."

The remaining two players began to dive in order to move faster in the air. They charged right for them, but Grey wasn't scared. He didn't know a lot about Lam's squad, but he did know they weren't at their best in open combat. They excelled in their mazes of builds. Lam and Pilar landed alive and began to box in.

"Push!" Grey ran for the structure, determined to get them down before they had a chance to heal. He shot the walls so Lam and Pilar would have to keep rebuilding them instead of using whatever shields or bandages they might have.

Finn knocked down Lam.

"One more!" Grey's SMG needed a reload, so he switched to his AR instead to keep up the pressure.

With all the fire focused on Lam, she couldn't keep the walls up to protect herself. It was Hazel who got the last elimination, and Grey's screen lit up with *Victory Royale!*

"Nice job, guys," Grey said before they were transported back to the battle warehouse. They had won half their games over the past two days, and that was no small feat. Their ranks within the squad would be determined by eliminations, and thus Kiri usually got the number-one rank.

Grey stared at the rankings as the Admin appeared. Kiri was now above Tristan, knocking him from the top ten. Grey was ranked twelve and Hazel was thirteen. Finn was a bit further back at rank twenty.

"Day Forty-Two of Battles has come to an end," the Admin said. "Please note that after your resting period, the new patch will be applied. As a reminder, I will now recite the incoming changes . . ."

Grey tried to listen carefully to all the modifications the weapons would undergo, but there were so many it was hard to keep track. The basic gist was that SMGs and explosives would be the strongest weapons, and ARs and shotguns would be nerfed. Grey didn't like that—the damage of the shotgun was often how he got eliminations.

After the Admin left, everyone began to organize into their squads like usual. But this time Grey noticed several veteran squads had grouped up. They were huddled together, and it looked suspicious.

"I have a bad feeling about that," Grey said as he nodded over to them.

"Yeah, mate," Kiri said. "I don't think they like us winning."

"What're they gonna do about it?" Finn asked. "Talking won't help them beat us."

"You wanna bet?" Hazel looked at the group, her arms folded across her chest. "This Battle Royale isn't just about what happens in game—it's also about what happens right here in this lobby."

Just as Hazel finished her sentence, Zach jumped up on table and cupped his hands around his mouth. His voice carried across the warehouse as he said, "Yo, everyone! Listen up!"

All the players in the warehouse turned. Grey wanted to leave, but he felt like whatever Zach had to say involved Grey's squad.

"I'm issuing a bounty!" Zach pointed at Grey's squad. "Any of y'all who eliminate people in that squad, we'll give you private lessons on how to play so you have better chances next season. Every elimination will get you one practice."

Grey's eyes widened, but it was Finn who said, "You can't do that!"

"Yeah, we can," Zach replied.

"Not this again . . ." Lam shook her head and walked right out of the warehouse with her squad. A few more people not in her squad followed her. At least some of the veterans didn't want to play dirty. Grey respected Lam even more for that.

"That's so unfair," Kiri grumbled.

"You know what's not fair?" It was Vlad who spoke this time. Grey had never heard him talk, but apparently all Grey's recent victories were enough to tilt Vlad as well. "It's not fair that a bunch of noobs who haven't paid their dues are in the top fifteen."

"Will all of you let them get away with this?" Yuri yelled to the crowd. "How many of you deserve to go home sooner than them?"

The crowd sounded like they agreed with the veterans, and Grey began to fear for their ranks. They had gotten so close, but if all the casual players started being serious about taking out Grey's squad . . .

They'd have no chance.

CHAPTER 7

For the first time in a while, most of the players rushed to the practice area. It appeared that Zach's incentive of lessons in exchange for eliminations on Grey's squad was enough motivation for people to start taking the game seriously again.

Grey loaded up on weapons and materials for practice, but he couldn't help noticing that everyone was lingering and watching them. "They're going to follow us, aren't they?"

"Ugh, probably. Everyone's a spy now," Hazel said as she loaded up on explosives. She had unofficially become their pro at all things exploding, and it actually worked out well. She had better aim with grenades than any of them, and she was good at placing and detonating C4 at the right time.

"How are we supposed to practice with everyone watching us?" Kiri asked. "They'll learn our play style."

"Doesn't even matter with the weird spectator mode in here," Finn grumbled. "The second one of them is dead, they'll tell their whole squad where we are because they can spectate us. Everyone else might be able to figure it out from there if they organize and know which group is hunting us in which locations."

"That's true." Grey let out a long sigh. "It doesn't even feel worth it to practice."

While Grey had faced being trolled and betrayed and underestimated, this new bounty on their heads felt downright dirty. He couldn't understand how Zach and the rest of them could stoop that low just to keep Grey and his squad down. All he wanted was a fair chance—the game was already hard enough without the players putting roadblocks in the way.

"So we're not practicing?" Finn asked. "I think we still should. It doesn't matter if all those scrubs come for us. We can beat them. We beat them all the time."

Kiri shook her head. "Some of them aren't scrubs, Finn. Some of them are pretty good players who are dying early because they want to stay in the game longer. They'll want extra training for when they want to get out."

"I see . . ." Finn looked to both sides, eyeing everyone who loitered in the practice warehouse. "Well, this sucks."

"You know what?" Grey said. "You guys can practice or not, but I need to think if there's any way we can get around this."

Hazel nodded. "If anyone can think of something, it's you."

Grey was thrown by the compliment, but he appreciated it even more coming from Hazel. She never said anything she didn't mean.

Waving goodbye to his squad, Grey walked away from the practice area. As he did, all the things he carried disappeared from his inventory. He walked toward the cabins, where it was quiet outside for the first time in a long time. Usually people hung out there, but today they were all back to practicing. He was glad for the extra quiet. Maybe his brain would come up with something to get them out of this situation if he rested in bed.

As he approached his cabin, Grey peeked in the window to see if anyone was in there. He wouldn't mind if Lorenzo or Tae Min were there, but if Ben and Tristan were inside, he'd have to go to his favorite spot in the woods instead. He definitely didn't want to see them after their squad leader just put a bounty on him.

Sure enough, Ben and Tristan were inside. They weren't resting, but standing in the middle of the room. It looked like they were arguing.

"Stop worrying about it!" Tristan said. "We need to focus on the top five. There's less than two weeks left."

"I can't help it!" Ben yelled back. "This isn't how I wanted to win! Imagine if we were in Grey's squad still."

"It doesn't matter how we win," Tristan said.

"I think it does." Ben looked at the ground, and Grey's insides twisted up because he could tell Ben didn't like what Zach had done. "We . . . could have won with Grey. And we would have done it fair and square."

"No, because the vets would have sabotaged him just like now," Tristan replied. "They won't let noobs have the top five—why do you think we've never gotten this far before? Because you always recruit noobs. I told you this side of the game was important. Don't back out now. We are this close to going home."

"I can't back out . . . It's not like Grey would take me back. His squad is full anyway," Ben said.

But the thing was, Grey would take Ben back if he could. As Grey listened to them, he still missed them in a way. Even if they had betrayed them. He knew they wouldn't do that under normal circumstances, but this hacked game was nothing near normal. It was nice to hear Ben didn't like the bounty, even if Grey knew Ben and Tristan would still stick with Zach's squad.

Grey couldn't kick anyone out of his squad anyway. They finally had the synergy they needed.

If only they could all go home. Grey would have loved to make that happen.

But the four in his squad, plus Ben and Tristan, would make six. So even if Grey could help everyone get to the top five, one person would be left out. Rank six must have been the hardest one to hold at the end of the season—so close and yet so far away.

Grey turned around and headed for the forest. While he had wanted the softness of a bed to rest in, the grassy ground would have to do. But as he approached his favorite spot, he saw Tae Min was already there.

"You're late," Tae Min said.

"Sorry?" Grey wasn't sure what else to do but to sit down at the barrier like the mysterious Tae Min who had taken him under his wing.

"You don't seem to be upset about the bounty," Tae Min stated in his matter-of-fact way.

Grey let out a tired sigh. "I guess I'm getting used to it. Every time I start doing well, someone shows up to pull me back down."

"Yes," Tae Min said. "But you always get back up."

Grey hadn't thought about it like that, but he realized it was true. There were so many times during the season when he could have given up. He could have accepted that he wasn't going to make top five this season. Yet he never stopped hoping and trying to succeed.

"Sometimes I don't want to get up," Grey admitted. "But people are relying on me now. I don't want to let them down."

"Don't get up for other people. Do it for yourself," Tae Min said.

Grey stared at Tae Min. He was always giving advice to Grey, and it always sounded so harsh. But eventually Grey would see the wisdom in it. "Why not get up for other people?"

"You'll only get bitter over time if you

feel like it's your duty to make other people happy." Tae Min paused, but his pensive look told Grey there was more coming. "In my real life . . . let's just say everyone expected me to do what they wanted. And I did. And they were happy, but I wasn't. I tried to tell myself their happiness would make me happy. Then I got stuck in the this game, and finally there was no one and no duty I had to answer to. It was . . . liberating."

"So that's why you don't leave?" Grey asked.

Tae Min nodded once. "Partly."

It wasn't the reason anyone had guessed, but Grey could see why Tae Min wanted to escape. "I think I'm doing this for myself. I really want to go home. I help the others because they can help me, too. I couldn't do it on my own like you do."

"You could, in time. But I hope you don't have to."

"Still not sure how I'll get back up from this one," Grey admitted.

"You'll figure it out," Tae Min said as he stood up. "I'll give you time to think about it."

"Okay. See ya around, I guess?"

Tae Min didn't turn back, but only held up a hand to give a small wave. The gesture felt warm, personal, for some reason. Grey couldn't quite believe it, and yet it felt like he and Tae Min were friends. Or at least as close to friends as Tae Min ever allowed someone to be.

Grey didn't have time to think about his friendship with Tae Min, though. He wasn't going to rely on the top player to give him the answers. Clearly Tae Min thought Grey could find them on his own. Grey wanted to live up to that expectation, so he tried to think of the best way to minimize the effects of the bounty put on his head. And right before another big patch, too.

The biggest issues were more people fighting them, which would take more resources and bring more risk of elimination. The other issue was that if anyone got eliminated, the rest of their squad could benefit by that person spectating Grey's squad and making it easier for them to hunt Grey down. He could see some of these players purposely losing early just to spy on them and get their location.

Grey stretched out in the grass and closed his eyes, trying desperately to come up with a plan. But nothing would come.

No matter how he framed it, the only answer was to eliminate every player who came for them.

Plus face the top twenty players if they ever met them. Maybe they could land in the less-popular areas to farm up, but those places often didn't have enough loot chests for a full squad. They'd come out under-geared. There was really only one place on the map that was remote and yet had enough decent gear for a full squad.

Lucky Landing.

It was out of the way, being on the southern-most part of the map. It often wasn't close to the first storm circle, making it hard to get to the safe zone.

"If we landed there . . ." Grey mumbled to himself. It wasn't ideal, but he had a feeling the players wouldn't immediately guess that they'd go there. And it would be hard for people to hike down there, which would give Grey's squad time to grab loot and materials before the fighting began. Even if the lower-ranked players landed there, Grey was now confident enough that his crew could beat them first.

Lucky Landing was worth a shot. But he'd keep that a secret, even from his squad. At this point, he was afraid to say anything out loud for fear that a spy would be listening.

CHAPTER 8

When the next day came, Grey could tell his squad was nervous. Other players eyed them as they gathered outside the cabins. They even followed Grey and his squad to the battle warehouse, sitting at nearby tables when Grey's squad sat.

Hazel let out a huff as she glared at the crowd. "Stalkers much?"

Some of the people who were staring at them turned around, as if they could pretend they weren't planning to play bounty hunters in today's battles.

"What're we gonna do?" Finn whispered.

"Change your skins every game," Grey said quietly. "Other than that, you're gonna have to trust me until we're in game."

Kiri nodded. "Obviously we can't even talk about our plans."

"They will choke us out of practicing at this rate," Hazel grumbled. "I'm so angry I could punch every single one of them. And then beat up Zach for doing this to us."

"Eliminate them in the game instead," Grey said. "Remember everything we've already worked on. That's all we can do right now."

Finn nodded. "Now I know why the actual game makes it so you can't talk to enemies. All this drama sucks the fun right out of it."

"Yeah." Grey hadn't heard many negative things about being here from Finn. This was the first evidence that the reality of this place was finally starting to sink in for his real-life best friend.

The day began in the usual way, with everyone being transported to the battle warehouse to stand in the ranked line while the Admin talked.

"Welcome to Day Forty-Three of Battles!" the Admin began. "Today is patch day. The game has been updated during your rest, and all aforementioned changes have been implemented on the island. If you notice any bugs, please notify me immediately after any battle by using the Report

Bug icon available in your vision selection. We will work quickly to correct any issues, if they be valid and not in line with the patch's intended working order. Good luck in today's battles!"

The Admin disappeared, and the countdown began. Grey readied himself for a day that would be filled with the most difficult battles they'd ever faced.

The second Grey appeared in the Battle Bus, he said, "We're going to Lucky Landing. No one goes there, but it's good loot. If people watch us after elimination, it'll at least take them awhile to get there, and we'll have time to get gear."

"Sounds like a good plan to me," Kiri said.

"Luckily you've never shown a preference for a certain place," Hazel said. "Some squads always land in the same area."

Everyone began to jump out of the bus, so Grey and his squad did as well to blend in. The bus crossed diagonally over the island this time, heading from the southeast to the northwest. It was a good bus for Lucky Landing. He watched the pathing of the people in the air, and it didn't look like anyone had followed them.

Yet.

"Six landing at Fatal Fields," Grey announced as he observed the nearby landscape. "One at Moisty Mire. Two Flush Factory. Those will be our first concerns if they come this way."

"Got it," Finn said.

"Only Fatal has a potential squad," Hazel said, "so that's the most risk."

Grey smiled. Though Hazel was still brash, her strategic thinking had improved a lot. "Definitely. And whoever survives Tilted Towers isn't far off, either."

"Let's get this going!" Kiri landed in one building, and Grey took the one next to her. Finn and Hazel also spread out. They had all learned that was the best way to gear up fast if they were the only ones who landed in an area. Each of them would fully loot a house and announce what kind of gear they had so they could split it up to their best advantage.

Grey landed in the smaller house with the brown roof, while Kiri was in the big one. Finn was just north of them, and Hazel had taken the riskiest position in the buildings at the northern edge of town.

After finding a blue shotgun, the brand new SMG that looked like a tommy gun, one small shield, and a bunch of ammo, Grey moved to another building with a red roof.

But the notifications began to concern him. There were way more people being eliminated from a great fall than usual. And it was easy to tell it was only one person in the squad.

Jamar had a great fall.

"Looks like your old squad is in on the bounty, too, Hazel," Grey said.

"Of course they are," Hazel replied. "Better hurry and farm up. Everyone is on their way now."

"Every building," Grey said as he broke down trees on his way to the next place. He'd gathered a good amount of brick already, but Lucky Landing wasn't a great place to get wood.

The storm was about to start, and Grey waited to see where the next circle would be. If it was in the north, they were destined to struggle the whole game. But it also might deter people from trying to venture south to get them. Grey wasn't sure which would be better, because either people would come for them or their enemies would wait at the storm's edge and pick them off.

The timer ticked down, and the game announced the two minutes and thirty seconds until the storm closed in on the first circle. Grey pulled up his map as he farmed more brick and metal. The circle was still over them for this game.

"They'll be coming to us," Grey said. "Let's push out of Lucky to get wood. Depending on the next safe zone, we'll either move back here or get in the circle."

"Okay. I'll take a sniper position in that big house at the northwest," Kiri said.

"Good thinking," Grey replied. There was one large building farther north in Lucky Landing, and Kiri ran inside there as Grey, Finn, and Hazel made their way to the trees surrounding the area. They had all learned by now not to fully knock down the trees because players could see them disappear from far away.

"We have incoming!" Kiri said as she took her first shots. "Northeast! Three!"

"Always assume they know where we are," Grey said as he turned his attention to the northeast horizon. "Even a less skilled player can down you with all that extra information."

"How should we use our explosives?" Finn asked. "I picked up clingers."

"I got a grenade launcher," Hazel added.

"Save them until we face tough players. Or if we get in a bad spot." Grey located the players pushing Kiri. He opened fire with his new SMG in hopes to draw their attention away from her, but they kept moving forward, using walls to protect their push.

"I need backup," Kiri said. "They're dodging so many of my shots!"

"Their eliminated teammate has to be spectating you," Hazel said, and she joined Grey in pushing for the house where Kiri was.

"Throwing one clinger," Finn announced.

Grey built ramps up even though they weren't focusing on him. He wanted to get up to Kiri as fast as possible and also provide another way for her to escape. She'd taken a couple hits and was getting low on health.

Dan knocked down Kiri.

"Hide!" Grey said as he reached a closer range on his opponents. He pulled out his shotgun and aimed. The number was yellow, indicating a head shot, but it only did sixteen damage. "What the—?"

Grey rushed to switch to his new SMG, but it left him open to taking a few hits. Hazel used walls to protect him, while Finn announced that he was using the rest of his clingers to save this fight. He managed to knock down all the enemy players, and they gave up their loot as they were eliminated. It was a good thing, too, because they had med kits and big shields to replenish Grey's and Kiri's health bars. Hazel went to revive Kiri as Grey healed himself.

"Dude," Grey said. "My head shot with the shotgun only did sixteen damage!"

"Seriously?" Finn said. "That can't be. That's crazy low."

"That's what it said," Grey insisted. "If the shotguns are that bad now . . ."

"Maybe it's a bug," Kiri offered. "You could report it after this battle."

"True." Grey wasn't sure if it was a bug or it was the nerf from the patch, and he was afraid to use it again in a clutch play and get in trouble like this time. But he didn't have time to think more about it because more shots came their way. And worse, the sounds of a rocket launcher backed up the rapid SMG fire. "Get inside!"

They all went deeper into the house to avoid the damage, but more rockets came their way. Grey and his squad fled back to the main area in Lucky Landing just as the next storm circle appeared on the map.

This time, Lucking Landing was outside of it. They needed to make it up to the Fatal Fields or move into Moisty Mire area to survive.

"I have a bad feeling about this . . ." Kiri said.

Grey wouldn't say it out loud, but he did, too.

CHAPTER 9

The next squad followed them too precisely not to be guided by an eliminated spectator. It frustrated Grey, but he also hoped he might be able find a way to use this to his advantage. Right now it was too hectic, but maybe by next game he'd have a better idea.

"They're right behind us," Grey said. "Anyone pick up traps?"

"Me," Kiri said. "Three."

"Place them as we run. Maybe it'll slow them down if we get lucky." Grey ran into another building, still using walls to block off their escape. "If they get hit, turn and fight."

"Putting on ceilings," Kiri reported as the mechanical sound of the first spike trap signaled she'd placed it. The enemy would probably hear it too, though maybe not through all their shooting and breaking down of walls.

As they made it through the building, Grey heard more shots in the distance. It was at least another squad, if not more. He couldn't tell if they were fighting each other or trying to take sniper shots on his squad. At least not until Hazel took a big chunk of damage.

Grey used more of his materials to block the damage, but the shots kept coming and he was running out of things to build with. "Finn, take over building, I'm almost out."

"Gotcha," Finn said as he replaced a broken wall just in time.

Kiri knocked down Rosita.

That had to have been a trap going off. Grey immediately turned to the building they just came from. "Get that player eliminated! Hazel, hold off the others with your 'nades!"

"On it!" Hazel pulled out the grenades and launched them over the wall at the incoming squads.

Grey and Finn rushed the building with Kiri right behind. It was the second trap that had caught Rosita, and now there was a box in the area as her squad mates tried to revive her. Grey used his new SMG to burst down the wall, and then he switched to his shotgun and hoped for the best. He took a shot right at Rosita, and—

"Ten damage!" Grey yelled.

Kiri eliminated Rosita.

"My shotgun did twenty-five on a headshot, what?" Finn said as he switched to his AR and kept firing. "That is a massive nerf if it's not a bug."

Kiri eliminated Diana by head shot.

"The hunting rifle still seems the same," Kiri said. "Guess it's not really a shotgun, though."

"Good to know." Grey used his new SMG to finish off the last person. This new weapon was pretty good. It didn't have to reload as often as the other SMGs, and the damage was high.

By the time they picked up the loot, it was clear that Hazel was in need of backup. Instead of running back, Grey pushed forward through the building to flank the enemies. He had to hope that whoever was spying was spectating Hazel and not him.

"You better be flanking," Hazel said. "And not leaving me for dead."

"Of course I'm flanking!" Grey used the last

of his materials to build a ramp so they had a better view of the enemies. There were five in total, so it had to be a three-person squad and a duo. They weren't fighting each other but instead going for Hazel. It made Grey want to scream at how unfair it was. How did this not qualify as cheating? Maybe they weren't exploiting an in-game mechanic, but they were exploiting the spectator mode.

. . . Except he'd done it, too.

Not often, but when his squad mates died, they would also scope out the enemies for his team. He'd never purposely had someone in his squad get eliminated just to do that, but he started to wonder how fair any of that was. Why did the Admin allow this kind of sabotage when she was so strict on other things?

Grey had a good shot on the enemies pressing Hazel, but just before he fired, walls appeared in his way. So the spectators had warned their squad of the flank. Grey built up more to see over the walls. Finn built another platform around to get a different angle on them. They were able to get a few shots to hit their targets, but these squads who would normally be easy to take down suddenly had a massive advantage.

The storm approaches in two minutes.

"Shoot," Finn said. "We need to go."

But there was no way. Hazel definitely couldn't escape the players on her, and even if they left her behind, Grey was certain people would meet them at the border of the next safe zone. "We need to get those five down before we go, so drop everything you have on them."

"Okay . . . clingers it is." Finn tossed all his remaining explosives into the enemy builds. Kiri built up higher to get a better sniper shot. And Grey kept spamming the enemy squads with his new SMG and AR. Finally, they turned their attention away from Hazel and onto all the damage coming from behind.

Just in time, too, because Hazel had no shield and only ten health left. She took cover, and Grey noticed her shield bar going up. She must have had small shield potions to drink.

Finn eliminated Sandhya.

You knocked down Warren.

"Shoulda focused on me, fools!" Hazel yelled through the comms. "'Cuz I didn't use all my 'nades!"

Hazel launched three more grenades into the fray, and two more players were knocked down.

It was pretty simple to finish off both squads after that and take their remaining loot, but there was one big problem—

They were about to get stuck in the storm.

"Move it!" Grey ran north, as did the rest of his squad, but the storm overtook them quickly. They began to take one tick of damage every second. It was the most dangerous for Hazel, who only had ten health when the storm hit them.

"Bandages here, Hazel!" Kiri said as she dropped some.

"Thanks." Hazel grabbed them and frantically healed herself as everyone else kept running for the safe zone.

Grey was sure they'd make it out of the storm, but he wasn't sure how long they'd survive after that. All of their health would be low, and more bounty hunters were definitely on the way.

Sure enough, as they approached the safe zone border, several people opened fire on them. Grey's squad tried to use walls to protect themselves long enough to get into the circle, but it only delayed the inevitable. They were eliminated before they made it inside.

The people who got the eliminations then did victory dances.

It made Grey mad, but he was also proud that they were able to make it to the top fifty even with so many people hunting them down. And they were able to eliminate eleven people with only their initial resources. It wasn't great, but it could have been worse. So he would take it for now.

CHAPTER 10

"Did you see that, Zach?" someone yelled the moment everyone appeared back in the battle warehouse. "My squad got the eliminations! You better make good on your promise!"

"Let's practice right now," Zach replied as he gave Grey a satisfied smile. "You can use your newfound knowledge to get them again in the next game."

Grey couldn't help but glare at Zach. When he first met the guy, Grey had thought Zach was nice. But this tactic wasn't just mean; it was cowardly. Grey wasn't going to let it slide this time. "Yeah, Zach needs you guys to do his dirty work because he can't eliminate us himself."

"Excuse me?" Zach's eyes went wide with

surprise, while several people in the audience went "Ooooooo" and some said, "Burn!"

"You heard me." Grey folded his arms, feeling far tougher than he probably should. Zach was five years older than him, much taller, but not much wider.

"This noob doesn't know his place!" Zach pointed at Grey, looking out at everyone. "He deserves this bounty on his head!"

Grey turned to their audience. Two could play this game. "You think he's really gonna teach you everything he knows? He's playing all of you. He'll teach you just enough. And even if you get good, he'd do exactly this same thing to you. Just watch—if he stays here another season, he'll throw a bounty on someone else that threatens him."

"All the more reason to make sure I get home *now*," Zach said, not even denying Grey's accusations.

Grey pointed at Zach. "Are you seriously going to reward him for being a bully? Is time spent here the only thing that earns you a pass home? What about skill? What about being a good person who plays fair and *earns* it?"

"The world ain't fair, kid," Zach said. "Get used to it."

"This isn't 'the world,'" Grey said. "This is a game. And in every game I've ever played, there are rules that make it fairer than life, to make sure people don't cheat, to give each player a chance to win."

"Yeah!" Kiri stepped in, her hands on her hips. "It's called good sportsmanship, ay? Maybe you're not breaking an exact rule, but you're ruining the game for everyone."

Zach shook his head. "No, I'm ruining the game for you guys. Only noobs think sportsmanship matters here. And that's why we'll be going home and you'll be settling in for the next season."

Grey balled his fists. He couldn't fight Zach here, but he wanted to beat him and his squad even more now. "I guess we'll see who's really going home. I don't think it'll be you. You don't have enough strategy to get through Lam's squad."

Zach narrowed his eyes. "Let's go train up our army, guys."

While Zach walked away, Grey made sure to glare right at Tristan and Ben as they walked by. They pretended to ignore him, but Grey knew Ben in particular could feel his disappointment.

Ben's face contorted in shame, and he kept his eyes on the ground. This wasn't how Ben wanted to play, and yet he'd gotten so desperate to escape that he finally caved to the idea that you had to play dirty to win. Tristan was steel-faced, but Grey felt like he was only hiding his guilt better.

As everyone cleared out of the battle warehouse to practice, Grey caught sight of Tae Min leaning on a wall. He was looking right at Grey with a smirk on his face. Then he walked off.

Grey was positive Tae Min approved.

That made him feel slightly better about speaking up.

"Dang, Grey," Hazel said. "How come you never spoke up like that when my old squad was trolling you?"

Grey sat at a table. He was tired. Not physically, since his body here wasn't real, but his mind was exhausted. "Because you weren't wrong. I wasn't good. I had a lot to learn. But now . . . I'm better at the game."

"Better?" Hazel sat down next to him. He would have never guessed she'd become anything close to a friend, but over the last week it felt like she'd become their big sister in the squad. "You're a prodigy, I think. In the real world, most people who play this game don't improve so fast. You've gone from ultimate noob sauce to practically pro level in like six weeks! You were . . . right—you can't judge a person on how they start out at a game. They might end up better than you."

Grey didn't know what to say when Hazel was being so nice. "But it doesn't even matter. It makes me so mad that we can't reach the top when we have the skill. I feel like I've made you all work for nothing."

"Maybe we should report Zach," Kiri said. "This is an exploitation of a game mechanic, isn't it? Maybe not in the normal sense, but nothing about this virtual reality is normal."

"It wouldn't hurt, would it?" Finn asked. "This is massively unfair."

"This can't be the first time someone put a bounty on another player," Hazel said. "It's so obvious. Wouldn't it have already been reported? Maybe the Admin already ruled it was fair play."

Grey shrugged. "I have no idea."

"You think anyone would tell us the truth if we asked?" Hazel sighed. "I doubt any of the veterans would after all that. They still seem to be on Zach's side."

Grey realized there was one person who would

know it all and would tell the truth: Tae Min. "I think I know who I can ask."

"Who?" Hazel asked.

Grey shook his head. "I'll be back in a bit."

Tae Min was probably already at the barrier waiting for Grey. That was why he was smiling before. So Grey stomped his way through the forest, trying to calm his nerves. He tried not to ask anything of Tae Min, but Tae Min was the only person who would give Grey a straight answer about this matter. And Grey needed to know.

Grey never imagined he would consider reporting another player—he didn't like to complain, and he knew what it was like to get reported unjustly—but this didn't feel the same as when Hazel had reported Grey. He wasn't mad he was losing. He was mad that the game felt rigged. If he was losing fair and square, he wouldn't dream of complaining about it.

Just like Grey guessed, Tae Min was already there. Grey didn't sit next to him. He was too restless to be still. "I have to ask you something. Is that okay?"

"I figured you would," Tae Min said. "Go ahead."

Grey sucked in a breath and gathered his

courage. "Has anyone ever been bounty hunted like this before?"

Tae Min raised an eyebrow. "What?"

"Like, in other seasons. Was anyone else targeted like my squad?" Grey tried to clarify.

"That's what you wanted to ask me?" Tae Min replied.

Grey nodded. "Why?"

Tae Min shook his head. "I thought . . . never mind. Yes, other squads have gotten bounties placed on them. Many of them you're fighting right now. Vlad and Yuri had one last season once they hit the top five—it cost them their spots home. Lam had one in season two before she started her own squad. Almost every season there has been at least one, if not more. I got a bounty on my head in season one, though it wasn't necessary as I had no intention of keeping my rank."

"Has it ever been reported?" Grey asked. "These players are exploiting the spectator mode after elimination. Isn't that cheating?"

"I think it is," Tae Min said. "But no, it hasn't been reported."

"Why not?" Grey couldn't believe bounties had happened since season one and no one had reported it. The whole idea was completely unfair.

"Well, I suppose the risk of reporting was more dangerous than the risk of not reporting . . ." Tae Min paused to think more on it. "If you think about it, someone who reports an issue must identify themselves *and* the perpetrator. And suppose the Admin rules that the bounty is fair—the victim will only be targeted more after that."

Grey cringed at the thought. It was already bad enough as it was, and he was certain not everyone was participating in the bounty because some people probably thought it was a dirty move. But if the Admin did say it was allowed, then there'd be even more players after them and they'd never make it to the top five. Not this season or any other one. There would be bounties all the time.

"But the Admin would have to rule it unfair . . ." Grey finally said. "This whole system would be ruined if she didn't."

"Would it?" Tae Min asked. "She claims this is a social experiment as much as it is a game. Maybe that sort of thing is part of their experiments."

"Maybe part of the experiment is to see if we'll accept unfairness when we don't have to." Grey stopped pacing as he said it, which was when he realized he was pacing in the first place. His own words sat with him. He wanted to believe that was the case.

"That's an interesting theory," Tae Min said. "I can't pretend to know what these game designers are after."

Grey squared his shoulders as he settled on his choice. "I'm reporting it. I think it's worth the risk."

Tae Min pursed his lips. "It could cost your whole squad their ranks."

"Our ranks are already doomed. Besides, if they leave I'll just manage solo," Grey determined. He turned around, already having made up his mind. He couldn't let this slide. If the bounty continued, he'd be stuck here anyway. So what was he losing by reporting Zach? His chances to go home were already lost if this continued.

As Grey walked back to the battle warehouse to talk to his squad, he accessed the reporting tool from an icon that was at the top right of his vision. It was small and easy to ignore most of the time, but right now it felt like it took up his entire field of view. As the semitransparent window popped up in his vision, his heart began to race. But he pushed forward before he doubted himself.

There were two options: Report Bug and Report Player.

Grey selected Report Player, and the next prompt was Player Name. Grey entered Zach. The report then asked what the player's offense was. Grey gulped as the reality of what he was doing set in, but he pressed forward. He detailed everything that had happened regarding the bounty. Grey reread his text once and then pressed the send button.

Report sent.

There was no turning back now. Either Grey was right that bounties were cheating, or Zach would be right and Grey would have to accept that he was here for another season.

CHAPTER 11

Grey's squad stared at him in shock when he told them what he did. Kiri's jaw dropped while Hazel shook her head back and forth.

Finn smiled smugly and was the first to talk. "Good for you, man. I hope they do something about it because it's totally unfair. In the real game, you can only spectate the person who eliminated you. Or you can watch your squad mates. That's it. This whole 'picking whoever you want to watch' thing opens up so much room for cheating."

"You know Zach will come after us twice as hard if you're wrong, don't you?" Hazel asked. "You put us all at risk without even asking us."

"You can leave my squad if that happens. I

only put my name on the report, not all of us," Grey said. "I won't feel bad. I just couldn't let this slide."

Kiri sighed. "I'd rather not leave you for dead. Let's hope you're right."

"Zach won't know until the end of the day when the Admin shows up," Grey said. "So let's make the most of these games and hope for the best, okay?"

"What else can we do?" Hazel looked the most upset about it, and Grey figured it was because she had been on the losing end of reporting someone for cheating. When the Admin ruled that Grey wasn't cheating, almost all the players who had been on her side turned against her.

"I'll take full responsibility for this, Hazel," Grey said in an attempt to comfort her. "You can disown me for this if you want."

"I just might . . ."

The next battle begins in thirty seconds!

The next four battles of the day did not go well. Grey had hoped his speech might convince some people not to hunt down his squad, but it didn't help at all. Even though he picked remote landing spots, people still hiked all the way across the map to take them down. Even though Grey prepared his squad as best he could, they couldn't fight off ten to fifteen players at once. Especially when those players weren't trying to eliminate each other until Grey's squad was down.

No matter how many good weapons they found, no matter how many materials they farmed, no matter how smart they played—it wasn't possible to win against this onslaught.

Every game, their ranking got worse. They barely made it out of the nineties in the fifth game. Grey was furious by that point and had zero regrets about reporting Zach.

The Admin appeared as they all stood in line. "I hope you enjoyed playing on the new patch. There have been seven bug reports registered for investigation. There has also been one report of cheating and game mechanics exploitation made by Grey concerning Zach—"

"What?" Zach yelled. "Seriously? You reported me?"

"We're supposed to report cheaters," Grey called back.

"I didn't cheat!" Zach said. "Everyone knows people do this, you noob."

"Doesn't make it right," Grey asserted.

"That's enough," the Admin said. "We will

investigate all issues and deliver all verdicts on these matters. Thank you for your observations. We will review these reports overnight and inform you of any changes made in the morning before the day's battles. The practice area has now been updated with the patch's altered equipment. You have the customary three hours to take advantage of that resource. This concludes day Forty-Three of Battles."

When the Admin disappeared, the entire battle warehouse went up in commotion. Zach charged at Grey, Zach's extra height towering over Grey as he yelled at him. "You think reporting me is gonna save you? You're dead meat now, noob."

"I don't care," Grey replied. "It's wrong. You all know it."

Zach put his hand on his chest. "And why do I get to pay for something everyone has done? If I get punished, *everyone* here should get punished!"

"It's one thing to watch in spectator mode after you're eliminated and report to your squad, and it's another thing to put a bounty on players." Grey folded his arms. "Not everyone encourages people to exploit a game mechanic in order to sabotage a squad."

Zach shook his head, but he didn't seem to have an argument for that. Instead, he stomped back to his squad, and they left the battle warehouse with several other people.

Grey wasn't used to staying away from the practice area, but it still felt pointless to go there until the Admin made a decision about the bounty. So Grey sat down right where he was. His mind was frayed from all the thinking and stress of the day. But all things considered, the confrontation with Zach could have been worse. He pictured Zach throwing punches at him and a brawl breaking out in the battle warehouse.

"You look dead," Finn said as he sat on the ground with Grey.

"I wish I could go to bed right now," he admitted.

"Go lie down. Try not to think about it," Kiri said. "There's nothing we can do until they decide, anyway."

"May as well take a break when we can justify it," Hazel added. "You'll want to practice us into the ground if the Admin comes back in your favor."

Grey couldn't help but grin a little. "Very true. We are so behind."

"Go chill, man," Finn said.

So Grey did. He tried to tell himself there wasn't anything else he could do. He'd done what he thought was the right thing, and that would have to be enough for now.

The next day finally came, and Grey had never wanted to see the Admin more than he wanted to see her now. He wanted to know if anything would change or not because he couldn't move forward with any plans until then.

Grey determined not to leave his cabin at all that morning, knowing that the game would teleport him to the battle warehouse at the appointed time. The Admin would address the bug and player reports first, so it wouldn't take long. He closed his eyes and waited for everyone else to leave the cabin so he could have time alone.

Three sets of footsteps headed for the door, but there was still one person there with him. Grey assumed it was Tae Min, and Grey waited for him to say something. But instead, he heard the person walk closer and then sit on his bed. Grey opened his eyes because he was sure Tae Min wouldn't do something like that.

It was Ben.

Grey waited for him to speak, but Ben sat there and stared at the ground. He looked upset, nearly in tears. Finally, he said, "I'm sorry."

"I know," Grey replied.

"We should have had more confidence in you." Ben wrung his hands. "I thought I wanted to win at any cost . . . but this doesn't feel like winning. I hope the Admin sides with you. It should at least be a fair fight."

Grey pulled himself up to sitting. Ben still hadn't looked at him, but Grey found himself smiling. He missed Ben and Tristan, even if they had betrayed him. "Thanks. You know I still want you to get home, right? Even if I'm fighting to get myself there, too."

Ben nodded. "I wish we all could go home. They should only take people here who want to be here."

"Seriously," Grey said.

Before any more could be said, Grey's vision went to the familiar black that indicated he was being teleported somewhere. He appeared in the battle warehouse, and he gulped as the Admin appeared to start the day and deliver the verdicts for the reports made yesterday.

"Welcome to Day Forty-Four of Battles!" the Admin said with a smile. "We had several bug reports yesterday concerning the new patch, many of which involved the damage output of some shotguns. The developers have concluded that these shotguns are working as intended, and the reduced damage is accurate to the patch changes."

Almost everyone in the warehouse groaned at this. Grey would have if he wasn't so nervous about the next topic on the list, because the shotgun nerf was a game changer for sure. And not in a good way.

The Admin continued. "As for the player report made concerning Zach and the misuse of post-elimination spectator mode, the developers have been reviewing footage from every season regarding the concept of bounty hunting. We would like to note that, though this report was made directly against Zach, that the accuser urged us to review the history of the concept and the overall flaws of a spectator mode that allows all the eliminated players to choose who they spectate while the rest of the battle plays out. It has been determined that the nature of spectator mode opens up too many unfair opportunities for all players and thus impedes the fairness of our competition."

Players gasped at the announcement, and Grey's heart soared with relief, though the admin wasn't finished yet. This meant he would at least have a fair chance, and that was all he wanted.

"Spectator mode has now been altered to the way it works in the real word—you may only spectate squad members or the person who eliminated you," the Admin declared. "As far as punishment for using spectator mode in an exploitive manner, we have determined that no one will be disciplined as it is ultimately our fault for allowing a flaw like this to taint our competition. All currently declared bounties must be revoked, and any future ones declared will be punished by losing ranks. Good luck in today's battles!"

Battles will begin in thirty seconds!

"Sweet as, mate!" Kiri said over the squad comms the moment they appeared in the Battle Bus. "I'm so relieved they sided with you!"

"Me too," Grey said as he looked at the map for the bus's path. It was flying over the southern half of the map. "I'm feeling lucky after all that. So, Lucky Landing?"

Hazel let out a short laugh. "Sure, why not?"

"After having the guts to report Zach," Finn said, "you go wherever you want, dude."

"Dropping in three, two, one, go!" Grey jumped from the bus as it flew over Greasy Grove, but they would be able to get to Lucky Landing from there just fine.

Like usual, many people flew toward Tilted Towers and Pleasant Park, while some were landing right there in Greasy Grove. Grey could tell some players were also on the way to Lucky Landing, so Grey's squad needed to be ready for fights right away.

"Looks like we have a 'grab the first weapon you see' situation on our hands," Finn said as their squad and at least two others landed.

"We got this," Hazel said. "Lucky is our turf. At least they're only here because of the bus path and not because they can spy on us."

"Yup," Grey said. Since several enemies landed on the roofs, Grey went low and took to the first floor of a building. There was a shotgun, and while he didn't want such a weak weapon, it was better than nothing. Especially when he could hear footsteps. "Play it smart, guys. Don't take a fight that puts you in a bad position."

Grey ran to another room with a chest to

open. Out popped an AR, a trap, and small shield potions. He used the two potions to give him more protection, and then he began to break down the furniture for material to build with.

The footsteps grew louder—and there were definitely more than one set—so Grey decided to place his trap on the ceiling just in case the enemies charged him.

"Need backup," Finn said as shots echoed through the area.

"I'm close," Hazel said. "Hold on."

Grey wanted to help, but he had his own situation to deal with. Two enemies appeared and took shots at him. Before he could put a wall up, he lost his shield to the damage of a couple shots. "Two on me: one with a pistol and the other with a shotgun. Can probably handle it."

"I'll work my way there just in case," Kiri said. "My house was clear."

Grey didn't have enough materials to keep building through the damage, so he needed them to come in and take damage from his trap. He let the wall fall and used the shotgun first in hopes to get a good amount of damage on one of them. He hit one, but it wasn't half as much as usual for an up-close shot. He switched to the

AR, jumping up and down as he shot in hopes to avoid damage.

Finn eliminated Lorenzo.

Hazel eliminated Julio.

"Me and Hazel are good," Finn said. "But there are at least two more between us and you, Grey."

"Get them if you can. Don't worry about me." Grey took one more shot before he ran through the next doorway. He hoped, with his health so low, that they would follow in the hopes of getting the elimination.

They did.

Grey eliminated Sydney.

Grey eliminated Forrest.

Those two were in a squad that ranked in the seventies for the most part, so Grey knew they could deal with the others still there. He took their loot, though their weapons weren't much better than his own.

Kiri's avatar appeared just after. "All that running for nothing."

"Sorry," Grey said. "Four more to go, though."

Finn and Hazel were able to eliminate the rest of Lorenzo's squad, since Coco and Selena were split from each other. Kiri and Grey got the other two. They had plenty of time to loot the rest of Lucky Landing before the first storm started. Overall, it was a good start and much better than being hunted down like yesterday. It almost felt easy to play after that, which made Grey feel confident.

"Let's patrol the western storm border for people moving in," Grey said. The next storm circle favored them, so they were in a good position to be aggressive.

"Are you sure?" Kiri asked. "The stronger squads will probably be coming from that side, like whoever survived in Tilted."

"Better to get them when they're weak from the storm," Finn pointed out.

Tae Min was lost in the storm.

"What? How would he die in the storm?" Hazel said in surprise.

Grey knew. Tae Min was starting the process of tanking his rank, but Grey didn't mention that. Everyone would figure it out soon enough.

It was a strange relief, since Tae Min was always a threat you had to look out for. Now Grey could concentrate on the enemies right in front of him instead of worrying about getting sniped.

And that was a good thing, because as they approached the storm's border, there were two squads already fighting.

Tristan knocked down Hans.

"Zach's squad!" Finn said.

Grey was ready for some revenge. "Let's get them."

CHAPTER 12

Grey's squad couldn't have had a better chance to take out Zach's squad early. They were probably already weak from the storm, and they would be starved of materials since they were already fighting Hans's team.

"Kiri, break down their walls while we go in. Snipe when you have an opening," Grey said as he began to ramp up. "Dropping a bounce pad."

"Woohoo!" Finn cheered as he immediately used the bounce pad Grey placed on the wall he built.

Both enemy squads had seen them and started building defense walls, which Kiri took out in between taking sniper shots. Grey landed on the right side of the structure, while Finn took the middle, and Hazel took the left side. They had flanks on every side. It was almost too easy to take out all the remaining players in both Hans's and Zach's squads.

Grey eliminated Zach.

As that last notification appeared in Grey's vision, he had to admit it felt good. He was glad no one got punished for exploiting spectator mode, but it didn't hurt to exact his own revenge on Zach.

"We got this victory," Finn said with too much confidence.

"Pretty sure Lam's squad is still up," Grey replied. "Don't get too confident."

"And I haven't seen them get any eliminations," Kiri added. "Which means they've been farming this whole time."

"We better get ready." Hazel was already breaking down the nearest rock formation for materials. And everyone else joined in gathering materials. A couple other players tried to come in from the storm, but Grey's squad was able to take them out.

The next storm circle would push them back closer to Lucky Landing, and Grey began to have flashbacks of their last fight with Lam's squad at the location. If they had already built up a base, it would be hard to get a victory against them.

"You think they landed in the north or the east?" Kiri asked.

"Not sure," Grey said. Lam's squad was still the hardest for him to read. He wanted to guess north because they might guess that the storm would go up there. It didn't this battle, but it was a safe move. They also might have gone east to Moisty Mire where there would be plenty of materials to farm and usually no one to contest the weapons. Since there were no notifications about their squad, that might have been a good guess as well.

The middle of the game was too easy. Grey's squad was able to take out whatever lower competition they came upon. But the longer the game went without sight of Lam's squad, the more nervous Grey became. Their biggest competition would only be more prepared for a long fight.

As the safe zone grew smaller and smaller, the player count dwindled quickly. The space within the circle only encompassed Lucky Landing and the areas just north and east of that. Finally, there were signs of Lam's squad in the notifications.

Lam eliminated Yuri.

Pilar eliminated Vlad.

That put them down to seven players remaining—just Grey's squad versus Lam's squad.

"They'll be in the center of the circle, huh?" Hazel said.

"Probably." Grey had been patrolling the boarders, eliminating people from their advantageous position in the south. Lam's squad must have sneaked in at some point and secured their favorite spot. They wouldn't have to move since the storm would keep shrinking the safe zone around them. Grey would be forced to push and face whatever traps Lam had devised for this battle. "Well, may as well go in—we know they're not coming out."

Grey ran for the center of the circle, which was just northeast of Lucky Landing out in the open. It wasn't hard to spot the massive base Lam's squad had constructed. Especially when sniper shots came right at them. Grey built walls for defense.

"Rocket launcher time?" Hazel asked. They had acquired the weapon all the way back when they eliminated Zach's squad, but Grey had been determined to save it.

He was glad they did. "Fire away. We'll take out whatever is left with C4."

Hazel began to fire rockets, but they were slow to reload and Lam's squad was quick to rebuild the holes in their defenses. Grey grew frustrated, but he and his squad kept up the pressure and hoped to burn through their materials.

"Finn, take the building for me for a second," Grey said as he switched to an SMG to save his own materials. He littered the walls with shots, but still they weren't able to damage a single enemy. The storm was closing in again soon, which would push them closer to Lam.

Grey decided they had better charge them now before his team risked storm damage. "Finn, be ready with that C4. We're going in."

"Ready!" Finn replied.

Grey charged the formidable base, using his materials to protect his squad and also build higher off the ground so they could get a better view of structure. Lam's squad shot from windows they would edit in the walls, but they would close the widows right after with their fast editing skills.

Once they were closer, Finn began placing C4 on the building. It would destroy the outside wall and any wall on the inside of that, not to mention everything above and below. There was no better way to root out players than C4.

When Finn hit the trigger, the explosions blasted so loud that Grey couldn't hear anything else.

Finn knocked down Trevor.

That was a good start, but Grey was hoping for more. The full face of Lam's base was exposed, and Grey shot at the first movement he saw.

Grey knocked down Pilar.

It was just Lam now, but Grey couldn't spot her. "Anyone got eyes on Lam?"

"Nope," Kiri said as she looked through her sniper scope. "I haven't seen her at all."

"Weird . . ." Finn said.

Grey did not like that. Not one bit.

That was when he heard the *click* of C4 being placed. Grey gasped as he realized it had to be from Lam. Somehow she'd sneaked below them while her squad mates distracted Grey. And Grey's squad was high enough in the air to take fall damage if the C4 didn't eliminate them in one hit. Grey was already running down the ramp when he yelled, "Run!"

But it was too late. The C4 exploded on his

teammates, and they all fell to the ground. The fall damage eliminated them.

It was just Grey and Lam now, but he kept running because he heard more C4 being placed. Suddenly he really hated that stuff. It was too powerful, especially in the end game. But he had used it, too, so he should have expected Lam to save some. She had even been smart enough to bait Grey into using his squad's C4 first.

Grey got hit, and his shield melted. He had to try and eliminate Lam now before he went down. Either he would hit the shot with his hunting rifle and take out all of Lam's squad or he would go down first.

He dropped a bounce pad on a section of the ramp that was still standing and flew into the air. He turned and took the shot.

Lam sidestepped.

He missed.

Lam spammed him with fire from the new SMG, and Grey was eliminated before he hit the ground.

"Ugh, so close!" Finn said. "Good try, dude."

Grey sighed. It never felt good to get so close to a victory just to lose in the last fight, but he would have to accept it. And at least it had been a fair fight.

When they all appeared in the battle warehouse again, his squad gathered around him excitedly. Kiri said, "Do we get to practice now? I've actually missed it."

Grey smiled. "Yeah, let's do it."

"Can we join you?" an unfamiliar voice said.

Grey turned, his eyes going wide when he saw who was there. It was Lam and her squad. Grey struggled to speak from surprise, but Hazel chimed in, "Yes, please!"

"We'd love to. Grey really admires your tactical skills," Kiri added.

Grey nodded. "It would be an honor, really."

Lam wore a smile that made dimples show, and she pushed her short black hair behind her ears. "It would be an honor to play with a squad who wants to keep the game a real competition. I'm not afraid to fight it out on the island without any extra tricks."

"Good, me either." Grey never expected something so good to come of his player report on Zach, but the chance to practice with Lam was well worth the whole bounty ordeal. This would take his squad to the next level for sure.